COCONUT

BY CRESCENT DRAGONWAGON
PICTURES BY NANCY TAFURI

HARPER & ROW, PUBLISHERS

Coconut
Text copyright © 1984 by Crescent Dragonwagon
Illustrations copyright © 1984 by Nancy Tafuri
Printed in the United States of America. For informa-
tion address Harper & Row, Publishers, Inc., 10 East
53rd Street, New York, N.Y. 10022. Published simulta-
neously in Canada by Fitzhenry & Whiteside Limited,
Toronto.

Library of Congress Cataloging in Publication Data
Dragonwagon, Crescent.
    Coconut.

    Summary: A young girl imagines what her life would
be like if she were the owner of Coconut, a hyacinth
macaw she has admired at a pet shop.
    [1. Parrots—Fiction   2. Imagination—Fiction]
I. Tafuri, Nancy, ill.   II. Title.
PZ7.D7824C6 1984   [E]   83-47691
ISBN 0-06-021759-6
ISBN 0-06-021760-X (lib. bdg.)

1 2 3 4 5 6 7 8 9 10
First Edition

For Nina, who has frequently
gone out on a limb for me

C.D.

For Nana

N.T.

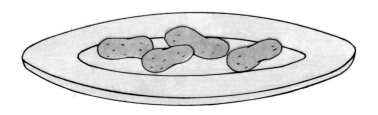

Coconut, a giant blue macaw, lives in Harvey's Aviarium,
a pet store on First Avenue.
When I visit Coconut,
he climbs up my arm,
balancing carefully with his ribbed gray feet.
He has a big black curved-over beak
and a small black curved-over tongue
and yellow at the base of his beak.
His bright eyes are sly and wise, shiny as marbles.
When Coconut blinks, his eyelids are yellow.

I wish Coconut were *my* bird.

We would live in a big apartment with lots of windows,

a red couch, and many trees in giant pots.

I would sleep on the red couch

with Coconut perched above me.

In the morning, when the sun shone through the windows,

lighting up the shiny leaves of the trees,

Coconut would wake me up.

He'd make little *mrrraw, mrrraw, mrrraw* sounds,

yawning his curved beak wide open.

He'd stretch each blue wing so hard

that all the blue feathers would stand up,

showing the gray down underneath.

I'd scratch the top of his head,
while he bent toward me, turning,
ruffling up his feathers so that I could get down deep,
right down to his warm, pink skin.
He likes being scratched there.
Prrraw, prrraw, prrraw.
Coconut would make his contented morning sounds,
and I would say, "Good morning, Coconut."

Then we would take a shower together.

He'd lean his head up

and blink in the water

and ruffle and stretch.

He likes the water,

like raindrops beating down on him,

because once he lived in the jungle, where it rains a lot.

When we came out,

he'd hang from the towel rack upside down by his feet

then grab it with his beak and hang right side up, watching me.

"Co-Co-Co-Co-Coconut!" I'd sing to him as I dried myself.

Mmmrrraw, mmmrrraw, mmmraw, he'd say to me.

At breakfast,

Coconut would sit on the back edge of his chair,

picking the nuts in their shells, one by one, from his plate.

He'd crunch a nut open with his smart, sharp beak.

He likes hard things in his mouth.

The golden day would stretch out in front of us,

full as a package that hasn't been unwrapped yet.

When I rode my bicycle,

Coconut would ride on the handlebars,

circling the silver chrome with his strong gray feet.

I'd go so fast,

Coconut's blue tail feathers would blow straight back.

I'd ring my bicycle bell and yell, *"Look out!"*

And Coconut would screech, *"Mrraw! Mrraw!"*

As we raced by, people would say,

"Did you see what I saw?

A girl on a bicycle

with a big blue parrot on the handlebars?"

Sometimes I'd stop and tell them,

"No, he is not a parrot.

He is a macaw. A hyacinth macaw."

But mostly I'd just bicycle faster.

And when I walked with Coconut on the top of my head,
people would say, "Did you see what I saw?
A girl walking down the street with a big blue parrot
on the top of her head?"

"Don't be silly, Roger, it was just one of those new hats."

"No sir, no madam, he is not a parrot, he is not a hat.

He is Coconut, my bird, and he is a macaw.

A hyacinth macaw, to be exact."

When we went to the beach,
we'd race along the shore
as the frilled waves rolled in and out.
My feet would pound fast on the sand
while Coconut flew above me,
screeching as he flapped his big wings up and down
in the moist salty air.

When I stopped, breathless,

he'd light on my shoulder,

and we'd just walk, quiet together,

against the ocean's roar and pounding.

We'd look for shells.

The perfect ones we'd save to take home,

but the broken ones Coconut could have for biting,

to crunch on and spit out,

to exercise his beak.

When we went for a picnic in the park,

I'd spread the tablecloth on the grass

while Coconut flew to the top of the tallest tree.

He'd perch there proudly,

looking down at me and screaming, *"Mmmmmrrrrraww!"*

Then I'd unpack the picnic basket and call,

"Coconut! Co-Co-Co-Co-Coconut!"

and my macaw would come swooping down to me,

to eat, from my hand, slices of an apple,

slice by slice, not greedy.

And I'd say to the round-faced babies in strollers

and the wide-eyed mothers,

and the little boys with balloons,

and the little girls on tricycles,

I'd say, "He's my bird."

"May I pat him?"

"Would you let him sit on my shoulder?"

"If he wants to," I'd say.

But Coconut would never really want to.

Oh, he wouldn't bite if a little boy patted him,

and he'd climb a lady's arm and perch on her shoulder,

but not for long.

Quickly I'd hear the quiet sound

of his giant blue wings beating the air

as he flew back to me,

landing on *my* shoulder.

Coconut would like *me* best.

If I left him for even a minute, he'd shriek,

"Aaaaarrrrrrwwww! Arrrrrrrwwww!"

"Sssh, sssh, Coconut," I'd say.

"See, I'm right here, it's okay."

And when we came home

with the shells we'd collected,

we'd put the picnic basket away,

and Coconut would lie in my lap

and rub his head into my side

and make soft *p-p-prrraww, p-p-prrraww* sounds.

It would be night by then, and my sleepy Coconut

would finally perch drowsily on the back of the red couch,

his eyes closed, his head tucked under his wing,

his long tail feathers drooping down behind him.

And when I lay down to sleep on the couch,

and the moon shone in the windows through the trees,

I'd close my eyes and smile,

knowing my giant blue bird,

my Coconut, sat dreaming above me.

But

Coconut is not my macaw.

Coconut would rather fly to Harvey at the Aviarium than to me.

He would rather eat apples from Harvey's hand than mine,

and he'll only stay on my shoulder for a little while when I visit.

As soon as he sees Harvey, he flies right back to him.

But someday,

I will have a hyacinth macaw of my own,

who will like me the best.

Someday we'll live in a big white apartment,

with many trees in giant pots,

just the two of us,

just me and my macaw.

I think I'll name him Sam.

SAM